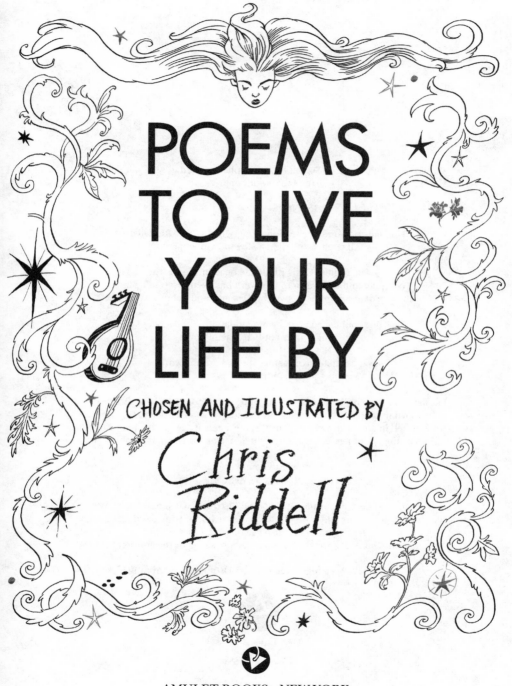

POEMS TO LIVE YOUR LIFE BY

CHOSEN AND ILLUSTRATED BY

Chris Riddell

AMULET BOOKS · NEW YORK

Cataloging-in-Publication Data has been applied for and may be obtained from
the Library of Congress

ISBN 978-1-4197-4121-0

First published 2018 by Macmillan Children's Books
an imprint of Pan Macmillan
20 New Wharf Road, London N1 9RR
Associated companies throughout the world
www.panmacmillan.com

Printed and bound in U.S.A.
10 9 8 7 6 5 4 3 2 1

Amulet Books are available at special discounts when purchased in
quantity for premiums and promotions as well as fundraising or educational use.
Special editions can also be created to specification.
For details, contact specialsales@abramsbooks.com or the address below.

ABRAMS The Art of Books
195 Broadway, New York, NY 10007
abramsbooks.com

Contents

Endings

An Introduction

The power of poetry is its ability to give voice to our experiences and emotions. We collect poems as we go through life. We read them at celebrations and at remembrances. We turn to them when we're in love and when we're heartbroken. Poetry connects us with one another and reminds us what it is to be human.

This is a collection of poems I have lived my life by. I vividly recollect sitting, as a very small boy, at the feet of an old soldier from the Great War. I remember looking up into a face ravaged by mustard gas and being told later that he had been blinded in an attack on the Somme—something I only understood after reading Wilfred Owen's devastating poem. I remember going through the looking glass as a young reader and into the tulgey wood where I encountered the whiffling Jabberwock. The swirling Gothic strangeness of Lewis Carroll's poem has stayed with me ever since. Later, at school, Shakespeare was drilled into me so that I could achieve exam success. Then, as a college student, I rediscovered him one magical midsummer's night, sitting on a cushion on the stage of the National Theatre in London. I remember having lunch with Ted Hughes early in my career and listening transfixed as he talked about his collection of poems called *Moon-whales* that he'd asked me to illustrate. I'll never forget meeting Roger McGough and Brian Patten for the first time at a rooftop party that featured flamingos. I once sat in a

train carriage opposite a sepulchral Nick Cave,
shared a stage in a tent with Neil Gaiman as he read
a poem about a witch, and drew live on a giant screen
to a sold-out crowd as Phoebe Bridgers sang about
beaches and pelicans.

I fell in love on Valentine's Day listening to the
songs of Leonard Cohen. I've felt the pang of my
children, grown up and independent in just the way
Penelope Shuttle describes, and the bittersweet
nostalgia for my parents that Charles Causley evokes.
I've found myself on a train from Hull to London,
reading Philip Larkin's famous poem for the first time
because of an inscription on a statue at the station.
I've paddled in the Indian Ocean with A. F. Harrold,
the bottoms of our trousers rolled, as he broke my
heart with his poem "I Miss You."

When I find poems like these, I like to write them
out and then draw around the words as I let their
meaning sink in. So, when compiling this anthology,
I asked for the poems to be given plenty of space so that
I could draw around them, directly onto the page. These
poems are certainly poems to live your life by. I hope
they speak to you as powerfully as they have to me.

CHRIS RIDDELL

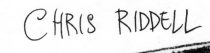

MUSINGS

"The isle is full of noises"
from *The Tempest*

Be not afeard. The isle is full of noises,
Sounds, and sweet airs that give delight and hurt not.
Sometimes a thousand twangling instruments
Will hum about mine ears, and sometime voices
That, if I then had waked after long sleep,
Will make me sleep again. And then, in dreaming,
The clouds methought would open and show riches
Ready to drop upon me, that when I waked
I cried to dream again.

William Shakespeare

"There is a pleasure in the pathless woods"
from *Childe Harold's Pilgrimage*

There is a pleasure in the pathless woods,
There is a rapture on the lonely shore,
There is society where none intrudes,
By the deep Sea, and music in its roar:

2

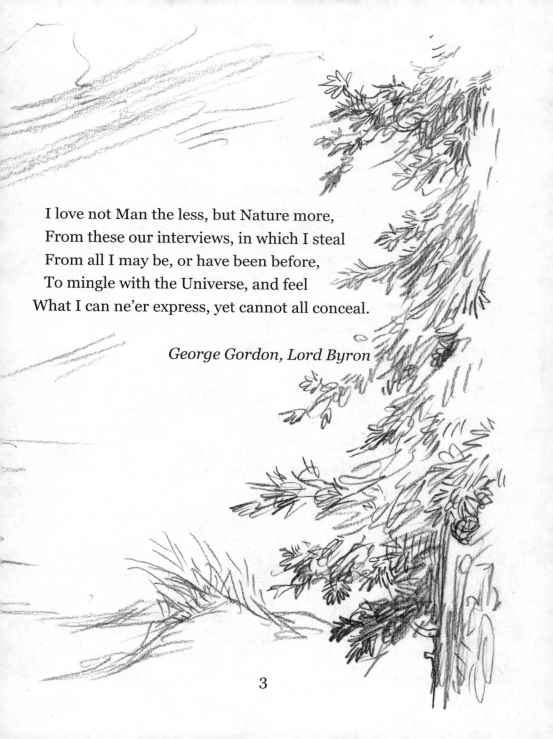

I love not Man the less, but Nature more,
From these our interviews, in which I steal
From all I may be, or have been before,
To mingle with the Universe, and feel
What I can ne'er express, yet cannot all conceal.

George Gordon, Lord Byron

3

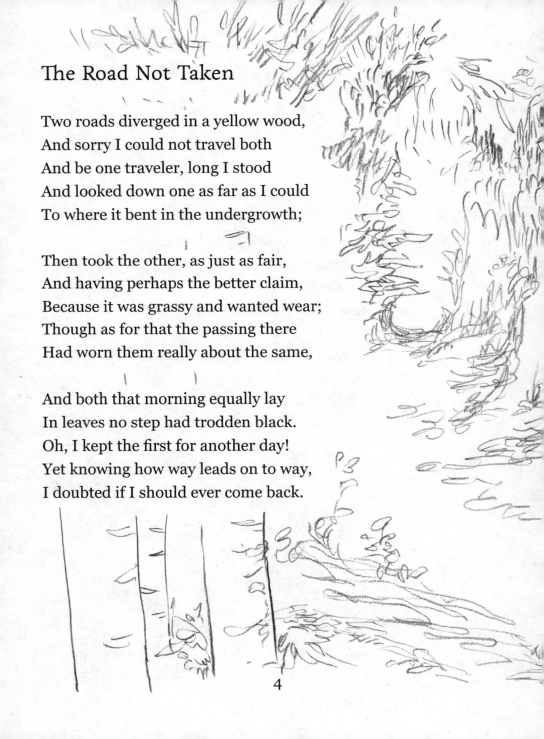

The Road Not Taken

Two roads diverged in a yellow wood,
And sorry I could not travel both
And be one traveler, long I stood
And looked down one as far as I could
To where it bent in the undergrowth;

Then took the other, as just as fair,
And having perhaps the better claim,
Because it was grassy and wanted wear;
Though as for that the passing there
Had worn them really about the same,

And both that morning equally lay
In leaves no step had trodden black.
Oh, I kept the first for another day!
Yet knowing how way leads on to way,
I doubted if I should ever come back.

I shall be telling this with a sigh
Somewhere ages and ages hence:
Two roads diverged in a wood, and I—
I took the one less traveled by,
And that has made all the difference.

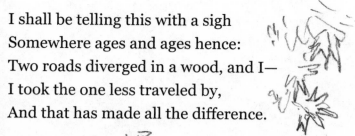

Robert Frost

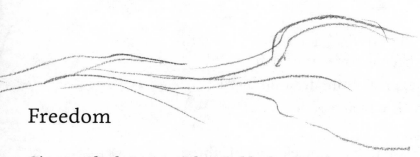

Freedom

Give me the long, straight road before me,
   A clear, cold day with a nipping air,
Tall, bare trees to run on beside me,
   A heart that is light and free from care.
Then let me go!—I care not whither
   My feet may lead, for my spirit shall be
Free as the brook that flows to the river,
   Free as the river that flows to the sea.

Olive Runner

Adlestrop

Yes, I remember Adlestrop—
The name—because one afternoon
Of heat the express-train drew up there
Unwontedly. It was late June.

The steam hissed. Someone cleared his throat.
No one left and no one came
On the bare platform. What I saw
Was Adlestrop—only the name—

And willows, willow-herb, and grass,
And meadowsweet, and haycocks dry;
No whit less still and lonely fair
Than the high cloudlets in the sky.

And for that minute a blackbird sang
Close by, and round him, mistier,
Farther and farther, all the birds
Of Oxfordshire and Gloucestershire.

Edward Thomas

9

Cargoes

Quinquireme of Nineveh from distant Ophir,
Rowing home to haven in sunny Palestine,
With a cargo of ivory,
And apes and peacocks,
Sandalwood, cedarwood, and sweet white wine.

Stately Spanish galleon coming from the Isthmus,
Dipping through the Tropics by the palm-green shores,
With a cargo of diamonds,
Emeralds, amethysts,
Topazes, and cinnamon, and gold moidores.

11

Dirty British coaster with a salt-caked smoke stack,
Butting through the Channel in the mad March days,
With a cargo of Tyne coal,
Road-rails, pig-lead,
Firewood, iron-ware, and cheap tin trays.

John Masefield

YOUTH

The Minister for Exams

When I was a child I sat an exam.
This test was so simple
There was no way I could fail.

Question 1. Describe the taste of the Moon.

It tastes like Creation I wrote,
it has the flavour of starlight.

16

Question 2. What colour is Love?

Love is the colour of the water a man
lost in the desert finds, I wrote.

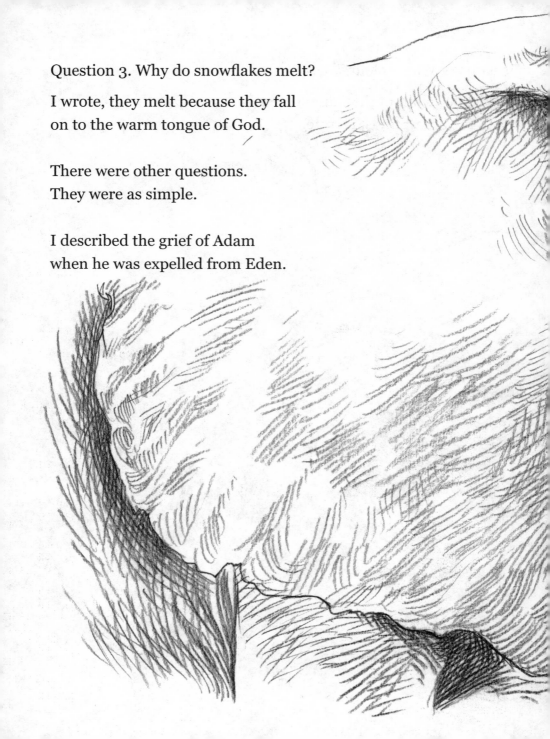

Question 3. Why do snowflakes melt?

I wrote, they melt because they fall
on to the warm tongue of God.

There were other questions.
They were as simple.

I described the grief of Adam
when he was expelled from Eden.

I wrote down the exact weight of an elephant's dream.

Yet today, many years later,
For my living I sweep the streets
or clean out the toilets of the fat hotels.

Why? Because constantly I failed my
    exams.
Why? Well, let me set a test.

Question 1. How large is a child's
    imagination?
Question 2. How shallow is the soul of
    the Minister for Exams?

Brian Patten

The Great Escape

Now, in the quiet of the studio at the bottom of the garden,
I remind myself of the unforgiving church pews,
My father's endless sermons and the wine gums
Bestowed on me by Mrs Stock
Like a benediction.

Of the hot tears damming behind my eyes
On the first day of school
When my mother let go of my hand
And how, an hour later, head below the table top,
I secretly wept.

Of the stewed prunes smuggled
Out from under the vigilance of the dinner ladies
In the pockets of my trousers
And dropped secretly into the flower beds
As, like a prisoner of Stalag Luft,
I planned my escape.

Chris Riddell

21

Thirteen

The boys have football and skate ramps.
They can ride BMX
and play basketball in the courts by the flats until midnight.
The girls have shame.

One day,
when we are grown and we have minds of our own,
we will be kind women, with nice smiles and families and jobs.
And we will sit,
with the weight of our lives and our pain
pushing our bodies down into the bus seats,
and we will see thirteen-year-old girls for what will seem like the
    first time since we've been them,
and they will be sitting in front of us, laughing
into their hands at our shoes or our jackets,
    and rolling their eyes at each other.

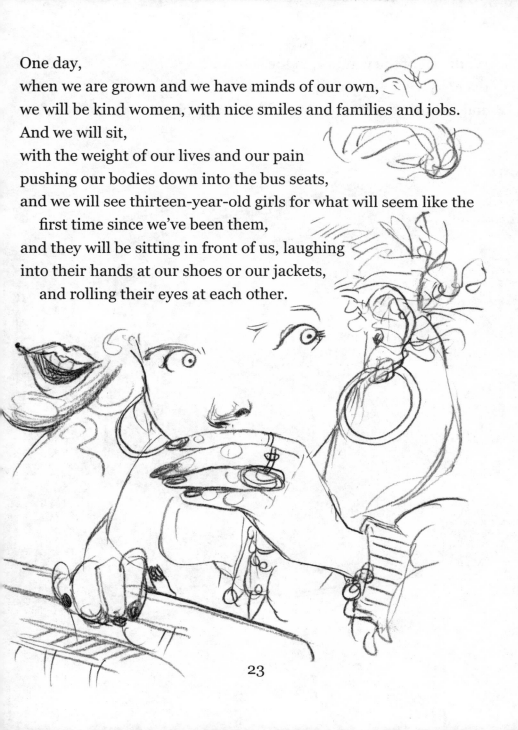

23

While out of the window, in the sunshine,
the boys will be cheering each other on,
and daring each other to jump higher and higher.

Kate Tempest

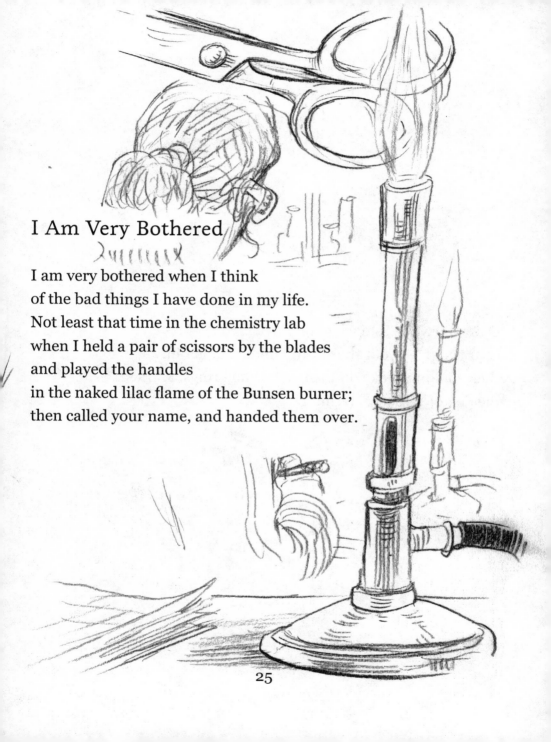

I Am Very Bothered

I am very bothered when I think
of the bad things I have done in my life.
Not least that time in the chemistry lab
when I held a pair of scissors by the blades
and played the handles
in the naked lilac flame of the Bunsen burner;
then called your name, and handed them over.

O the unrivalled stench of branded skin
as you slipped your thumb and middle finger in,
then couldn't shake off the two burning rings. Marked,
the doctor said, for eternity.

Don't believe me, please, if I say
that was just my butterfingered way, at thirteen,
of asking you if you would marry me.

Simon Armitage

27

Smoke Signals

I went with you up to
the place you grew up in
And we spent a week in the cold
Just long enough to
"Walden" it with you
Any longer, it would have got old

Singing "Ace of Spades" when Lemmy died
But nothing's changed, L.A.'s all right
Sleeping in my bed again, and getting in my head
And then walk around the reservoir

You, you must have been looking for me
Sending smoke signals
Pelicans circling
Burning trash out on the beach

One of your eyes is
Always half-shut
Something happened when you were a kid
I didn't know you then
And I'll never understand
why it feels like I did
"How Soon Is Now" in an '80s sedan
You slept inside of it because your dad
Lived in a campground in the back of a van
You said that song will creep you out until you're dead

And you, you must have been looking for me
Sending smoke signals
Pelicans circling
Burning trash out on the beach

I want to live at the Holiday Inn
Where somebody else makes the bed
We'll watch TV while the lights on the street
Put all the stars to death
It's been on my mind since Bowie died
Just checking out to hide from life

And you, you must have been looking for me
Sending smoke signals
Pelicans circling
Burning trash out on the beach

I buried a hatchet
It's coming up lavender
The future's unwritten
The past is a corridor
I'm at the exit looking back through the hall
You are anonymous
I am a concrete wall

Phoebe Bridgers

31

FAMILY

Walking Away

It is eighteen years ago, almost to the day—
A sunny day with leaves just turning,
The touch-lines new-ruled—since I watched you play
Your first game of football, then, like a satellite
Wrenched from its orbit, go drifting away

Behind a scatter of boys. I can see
You walking away from me towards the school
With the pathos of a half-fledged thing set free
Into a wilderness, the gait of one
Who finds no path where the path should be.

That hesitant figure, eddying away
Like a winged seed loosened from its parent stem,
Has something I never quite grasp to convey
About nature's give-and-take—the small, the scorching
Ordeals which fire one's irresolute clay.

I have had worse partings, but none that so
Gnaws at my mind still. Perhaps it is roughly
Saying what God alone could perfectly show—
How selfhood begins with a walking away,
And love is proved in the letting go.

Cecil Day Lewis

Outgrown

It is both sad and a relief to fold so carefully
Her outgrown clothes and line up the little worn shoes
Of childhood, so prudent, scuffed and particular.
It is both happy and horrible to send them galloping
Back tappity-tap along the misty chill path into the past.

It is both a freedom and a prison, to be outgrown
By her as she towers over me as thin as a sequin
In her doc martens and her pretty skirt,
Because just as I work out how to be a mother
She stops being a child.

Penelope Shuttle

Digging

Between my finger and my thumb
The squat pen rests; snug as a gun.

Under my window, a clean rasping sound
When the spade sinks into gravelly ground:
My father, digging. I look down

Till his straining rump among the flowerbeds
Bends low, comes up twenty years away
Stooping in rhythm through potato drills
Where he was digging.

The coarse boot nestled on the lug, the shaft
Against the inside knee was levered firmly.
He rooted out tall tops, buried the bright edge deep
To scatter new potatoes that we picked,
Loving their cool hardness in our hands.

By God, the old man could handle a spade.
Just like his old man.

My grandfather cut more turf in a day
Than any other man on Toner's bog.

Once I carried him milk in a bottle
Corked sloppily with paper. He straightened up

To drink it, then fell to right away
Nicking and slicing neatly, heaving sods
Over his shoulder, going down and down
For the good turf. Digging.

The cold smell of potato mould, the squelch and slap
Of soggy peat, the curt cuts of an edge
Through living roots awaken in my head.
But I've no spade to follow men like them.

Between my finger and my thumb
The squat pen rests.
I'll dig with it.

Seamus Heaney

37

Tissue

Paper that lets the light
shine through, this
is what could alter things.
Paper thinned by age or touching,

the kind you find in well-used books,
the back of the Koran, where a hand
has written in the names and histories,
who was born to whom,

the height and weight, who
died where and how, on which sepia date,
pages smoothed and stroked and turned
transparent with attention.

If buildings were paper, I might
feel their drift, see how easily
they fall away on a sigh, a shift
in the direction of the wind.

Maps too. The sun shines through
their borderlines, the marks
that rivers make, roads,
railtracks, mountainfolds,

Fine slips from grocery shops
that say how much was sold
and what was paid by credit card
might fly our lives like paper kites.

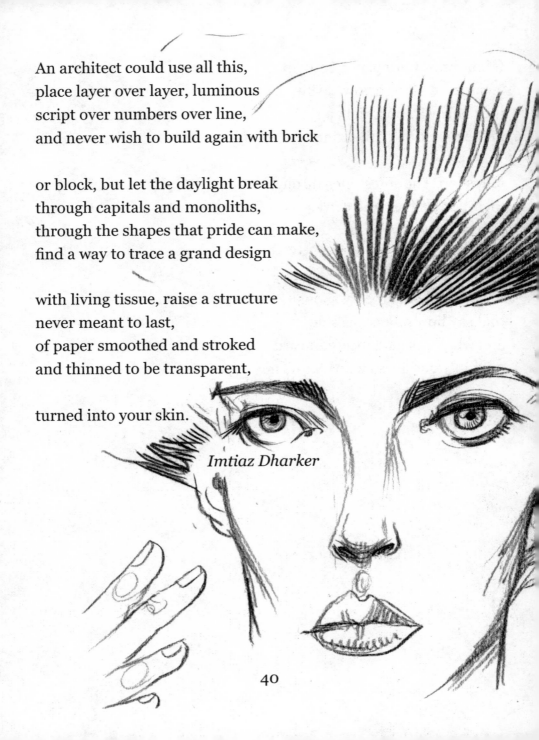

An architect could use all this,
place layer over layer, luminous
script over numbers over line,
and never wish to build again with brick

or block, but let the daylight break
through capitals and monoliths,
through the shapes that pride can make,
find a way to trace a grand design

with living tissue, raise a structure
never meant to last,
of paper smoothed and stroked
and thinned to be transparent,

turned into your skin.

Imtiaz Dharker

40

Eden Rock

They are waiting for me somewhere beyond Eden Rock:
My father, twenty-five, in the same suit
Of Genuine Irish Tweed, his terrier Jack
Still two years old and trembling at his feet.

My mother, twenty-three, in a sprigged dress
Drawn at the waist, ribbon in her straw hat,
Has spread the stiff white cloth over the grass.
Her hair, the colour of wheat, takes on the light.

She pours tea from a Thermos, the milk straight
From an old H.P. Sauce bottle, a screw
Of paper for a cork; slowly sets out
The same three plates, the tin cups painted blue.

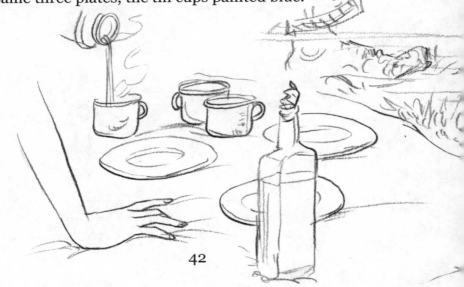

The sky whitens as if lit by three suns.
My mother shades her eyes and looks my way
Over the drifted stream. My father spins
A stone along the water. Leisurely,

They beckon to me from the other bank.
I hear them call, "See where the stream-path is!
Crossing is not as hard as you might think."

I had not thought that it would be like this.

Charles Causley

Safe Sounds

You like safe sounds:
the dogs lapping at their bowls;
the pop of a cork on a bottle of plonk
as your mother cooks;
the *Match of the Day* theme tune
and *Doctor Who-oo-oo*.

        Safe sounds:
your name called, two happy syllables
from the bottom to the top of the house;
your daft ring tone; the low gargle
of hot water in bubbles. Half asleep
in the drifting boat of your bed,
you like to hear the big trees
sound like the sea instead.

                Carol Ann Duffy

Bright Star

Bright star, would I were steadfast as thou art—
    Not in lone splendour hung aloft the night
And watching, with eternal lids apart,
    Like nature's patient, sleepless Eremite,
The moving waters at their priestlike task
    Of pure ablution round earth's human shores,
Or gazing on the new soft-fallen mask
    Of snow upon the mountains and the moors—
No—yet still steadfast, still unchangeable,
    Pillow'd upon my fair love's ripening breast,
To feel for ever its soft fall and swell,
    Awake for ever in a sweet unrest,
Still, still to hear her tender-taken breath,
And so live ever—or else swoon to death.

John Keats

45

LOVE

I Miss You

I miss you
Like the puddle misses the snowman it was

I miss you like the butterfly misses the caterpillar
Like the frog misses the tadpole
Like the penguin misses the warm egg

I miss you
Like my desk misses the tree it was before it was my desk

I miss you
Like the oak tree misses the acorn it grew from

Like the silence misses the song
Like the book misses the blank page

I miss you
Like the surprise misses still being a surprise

52

Like the sailor misses the land
Like the astronaut misses the earth
Like the grown-up misses being the child
Like the arrow misses the bow it's shot from

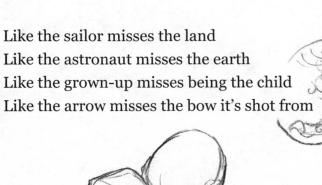

I miss you like I miss you.

A. F. Harrold

Something Rhymed

You're a gem, you're a holy cairn
You're a clattering shaw
You're a Tongland Bridge
You're a Solway Firth
You're a Big Water of Fleet
You're an old song, you're a valley

This feeling inside me could never deny me

You're a red deer of the forest
You're a wild goat of the moor
You're a Bladnoch malt,
A Whithorm Story, you're a friend, you're a glory.

Nothing old, nothing new, nothing ventured

Oh, you are definitely, so completely
The brightest girl of the glen.
You're a beeswing, you sing in a voice
Like a freshwater spring

Nothing older than time, nothing sweeter than wine

You are my Pinwherry,
You're my Loch Doon and Galloway,
You're my Gatehouse of Fleet,
You are philosophical, all Luce Bay,
And Whaupshill

Nothing I couldn't say.

Jackie Kay

There is a field

Out beyond ideas of wrongdoing
And rightdoing there is a field.
I'll meet you there.
When the soul lies down in that grass
The world is too full to talk about.

Rumi

58

Suzanne

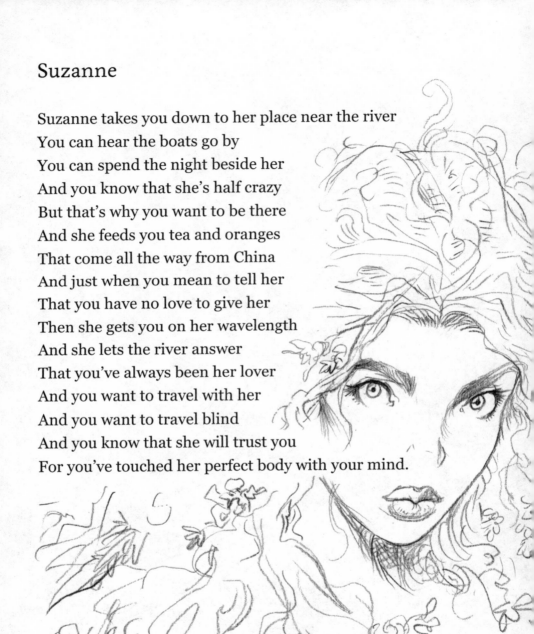

Suzanne takes you down to her place near the river
You can hear the boats go by
You can spend the night beside her
And you know that she's half crazy
But that's why you want to be there
And she feeds you tea and oranges
That come all the way from China
And just when you mean to tell her
That you have no love to give her
Then she gets you on her wavelength
And she lets the river answer
That you've always been her lover
And you want to travel with her
And you want to travel blind
And you know that she will trust you
For you've touched her perfect body with your mind.

And Jesus was a sailor
When he walked upon the water
And he spent a long time watching
From his lonely wooden tower
And when he knew for certain
Only drowning men could see him
He said "All men will be sailors then
Until the sea shall free them"
But he himself was broken
Long before the sky would open
Forsaken, almost human
He sank beneath your wisdom like a stone
And you want to travel with him
And you want to travel blind
And you think maybe you'll trust him
For he's touched your perfect body with his mind.

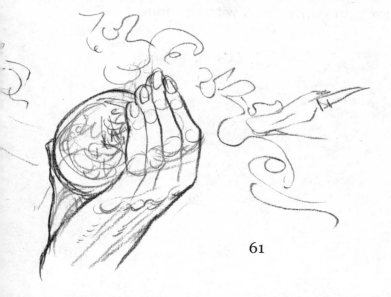

Now Suzanne takes your hand
And she leads you to the river
She is wearing rags and feathers
From Salvation Army counters
And the sun pours down like honey
On our lady of the harbour
And she shows you where to look
Among the garbage and the flowers
There are heroes in the seaweed
There are children in the morning
They are leaning out for love
And they will lean that way forever
While Suzanne holds the mirror
And you want to travel with her
And you want to travel blind
And you know that you can trust her
For she's touched your perfect body with her mind.

Leonard Cohen

He Wishes for the Cloths of Heaven

Had I the heavens' embroidered cloths,
Enwrought with golden and silver light,
The blue and the dim and the dark cloths
Of night and light and the half-light,
I would spread the cloths under your feet:
But I, being poor, have only my dreams;
I have spread my dreams under your feet;
Tread softly because you tread on my dreams.

W. B. Yeats

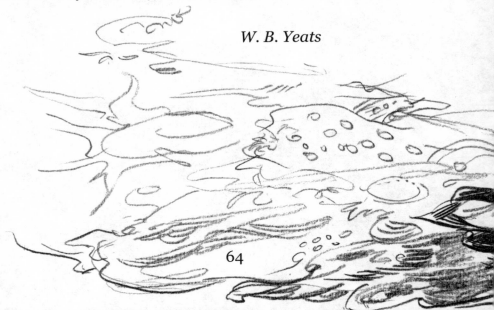

Sonnet 18

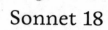

Shall I compare thee to a summer's day?
Thou art more lovely and more temperate:
Rough winds do shake the darling buds of May,
And summer's lease hath all too short a date;
Sometime too hot the eye of heaven shines,
And often is his gold complexion dimm'd;
And every fair from fair sometime declines,
By chance or nature's changing course untrimm'd;
But thy eternal summer shall not fade,
Nor lose possession of that fair thou ow'st;
Nor shall death brag thou wander'st in his shade,
When in eternal lines to time thou grow'st:
    So long as men can breathe or eyes can see,
    So long lives this, and this gives life to thee.

William Shakespeare

Invitation to Love

Come when the nights are bright with stars
Or come when the moon is mellow;
Come when the sun his golden bars
Drops on the hay-field yellow.
Come in the twilight soft and gray,
Come in the night or come in the day,
Come, O love, whene'er you may,
And you are welcome, welcome.

You are sweet, O Love, dear Love,
You are soft as the nesting dove.
Come to my heart and bring it rest
As the bird flies home to its welcome nest.

Come when my heart is full of grief
Or when my heart is merry;
Come with the falling of the leaf
Or with the reddening cherry.
Come when the year's first blossom blows,
Come when the summer gleams and glows,
Come with the winter's drifting snows,
And you are welcome, welcome.

Paul Laurence Dunbar

68

The Sun Has Burst the Sky

The sun has burst the sky
Because I love you
And the river its banks.

The sea laps the great rocks
Because I love you
And takes no heed of the moon dragging it away
And saying coldly "Constancy is not for you."
The blackbird fills the air
Because I love you
With spring and lawns and shadows falling on lawns.

The people walk in the street and laugh
I love you
And far down the river ships sound their hooters
Crazy with joy because I love you.

Jenny Joseph

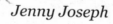

69

A Birthday

My heart is like a singing bird
    Whose nest is in a water'd shoot;
My heart is like an apple-tree
    Whose boughs are bent with thick-set fruit;
My heart is like a rainbow shell
    That paddles in a halcyon sea;
My heart is gladder than all these
    Because my love is come to me.

Raise me a dais of silk and down;
  Hang it with vair and purple dyes;
Carve it in doves and pomegranates,
  And peacocks with a hundred eyes;
Work it in gold and silver grapes,
  In leaves and silver fleurs-de-lys;
Because the birthday of my life
  Is come, my love is come to me.

Christina Rossetti

71

Valentine

Not a red rose or a satin heart.

I give you an onion.
It is a moon wrapped in brown paper.
It promises light
like the careful undressing of love.

Here.
It will blind you with tears
like a lover.
It will make your reflection
a wobbling photo of grief.

I am trying to be truthful.

Not a cute card or a kissogram.

I give you an onion.
Its fierce kiss will stay on your lips,
possessive and faithful
as we are,
for as long as we are.

Take it.
Its platinum loops shrink to a wedding ring,
if you like.
Lethal.
Its scent will cling to your fingers,
cling to your knife.

Carol Ann Duffy

Love Letter

I hold this letter in my hand
A plea, a petition, a kind of prayer
I hope it does as I have planned
Losing her again is more than I can bear
I kiss the cold, white envelope
I press my lips against her name
Two hundred words. We live in hope
The sky hangs heavy with rain

Love Letter Love Letter
Go get her Go get her
Love Letter Love Letter
Go tell her Go tell her

A wicked wind whips up the hill
A handful of hopeful words
I love her and I always will
The sky is ready to burst
Said something I did not mean to say
Said something I did not mean to say
Said something I did not mean to say
It all came out the wrong way

Love Letter Love Letter
Go get her Go get her
Love Letter Love Letter
Go tell her Go tell her

Rain your kisses down upon me
Rain your kisses down in storms
And for all who'll come before me
In your slowly fading forms
I'm going out of my mind
Will leave me standing in
The rain with a letter and a prayer
Whispered on the wind

Come back to me
Come back to me
O baby please come back to me

Nick Cave

The Whitsun Weddings

That Whitsun, I was late getting away:
    Not till about
One-twenty on the sunlit Saturday
Did my three-quarters-empty train pull out,
All windows down, all cushions hot, all sense
Of being in a hurry gone. We ran
Behind the backs of houses, crossed a street
Of blinding windscreens, smelt the fish-dock; thence
The river's level drifting breadth began,
Where sky and Lincolnshire and water meet.

All afternoon, through the tall heat that slept
   For miles inland,
A slow and stopping curve southwards we kept.
Wide farms went by, short-shadowed cattle, and
Canals with floatings of industrial froth;
A hothouse flashed uniquely: hedges dipped
And rose: and now and then a smell of grass
Displaced the reek of buttoned carriage-cloth
Until the next town, new and nondescript,
Approached with acres of dismantled cars.

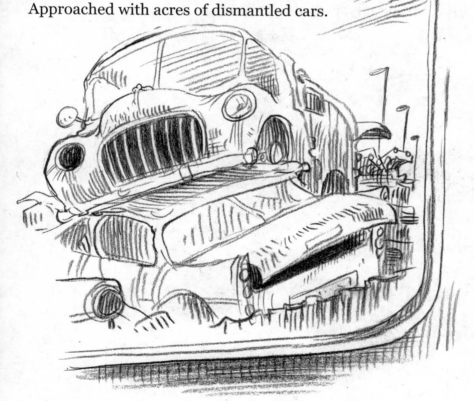

At first, I didn't notice what a noise
   The weddings made
Each station that we stopped at: sun destroys
The interest of what's happening in the shade,
And down the long cool platforms whoops and skirls
I took for porters larking with the mails,
And went on reading. Once we started, though,
We passed them, grinning and pomaded, girls
In parodies of fashion, heels and veils,
All posed irresolutely, watching us go,

As if out on the end of an event
    Waving goodbye
To something that survived it. Struck, I leant
More promptly out next time, more curiously,
And saw it all again in different terms:
The fathers with broad belts under their suits
And seamy foreheads; mothers loud and fat;
An uncle shouting smut; and then the perms,
The nylon gloves and jewellery-substitutes,
The lemons, mauves, and olive-ochres that

Marked off the girls unreally from the rest.
    Yes, from cafés
And banquet-halls up yards, and bunting-dressed
Coach-party annexes, the wedding-days
Were coming to an end. All down the line
Fresh couples climbed aboard: the rest stood round;
The last confetti and advice were thrown,
And, as we moved, each face seemed to define
Just what it saw departing: children frowned
At something dull; fathers had never known

82

Success so huge and wholly farcical;
    The women shared
The secret like a happy funeral;
While girls, gripping their handbags tighter, stared
At a religious wounding. Free at last,
And loaded with the sum of all they saw,
We hurried towards London, shuffling gouts of steam.
Now fields were building-plots, and poplars cast
Long shadows over major roads, and for
Some fifty minutes, that in time would seem

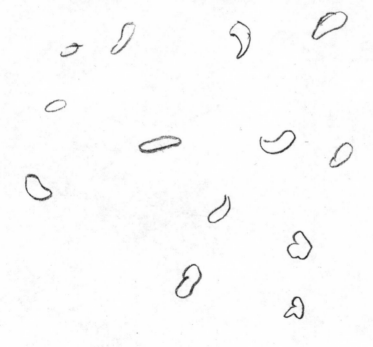

Just long enough to settle hats and say
  I nearly died,
A dozen marriages got under way.
They watched the landscape, sitting side by side
—An Odeon went past, a cooling tower,
And someone running up to bowl—and none
Thought of the others they would never meet
Or how their lives would all contain this hour.
I thought of London spread out in the sun,
Its postal districts packed like squares of wheat:

84

There we were aimed. And as we raced across
    Bright knots of rail
Past standing Pullmans, walls of blackened moss
Came close, and it was nearly done, this frail
Travelling coincidence; and what it held
Stood ready to be loosed with all the power
That being changed can give. We slowed again,
And as the tightened brakes took hold, there swelled
A sense of falling, like an arrow-shower
Sent out of sight, somewhere becoming rain.

Philip Larkin

85

IMAGININGS

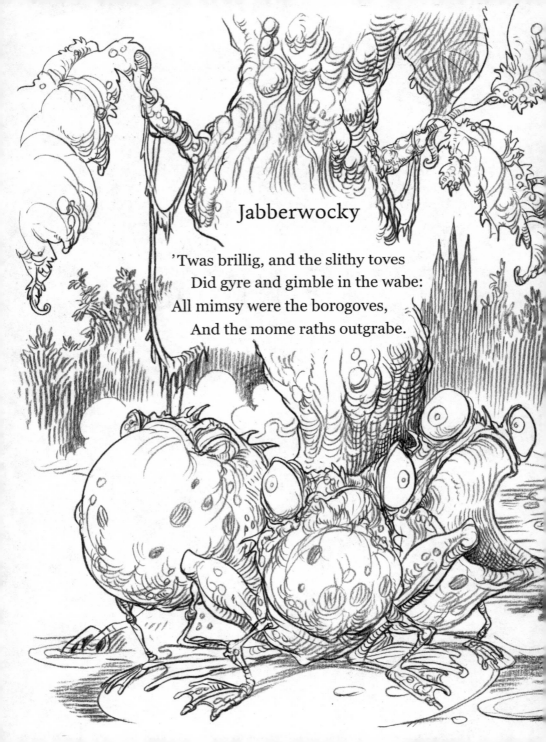

Jabberwocky

'Twas brillig, and the slithy toves
   Did gyre and gimble in the wabe:
All mimsy were the borogoves,
   And the mome raths outgrabe.

"Beware the Jabberwock, my son!
    The jaws that bite, the claws that catch!
Beware the Jubjub bird, and shun
    The frumious Bandersnatch!"

90

He took his vorpal sword in hand;
    Long time the manxome foe he sought—
So rested he by the Tumtum tree
    And stood awhile in thought.

And, as in uffish thought he stood,
The Jabberwock, with eyes of flame,
Came whiffling through the tulgey wood,
And burbled as it came!

92

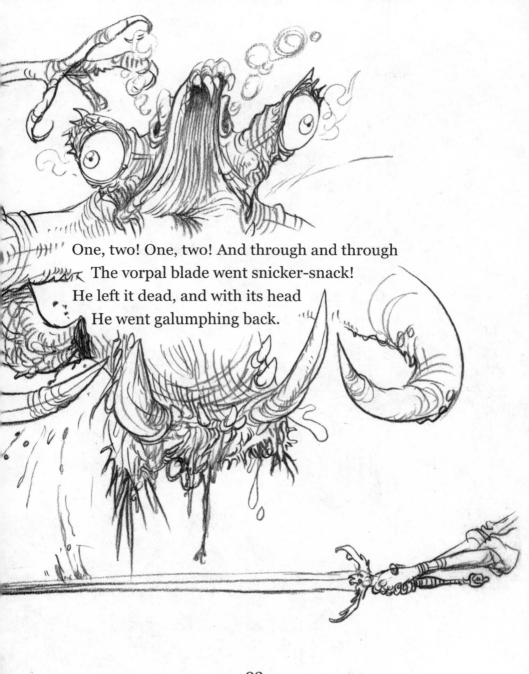

One, two! One, two! And through and through
  The vorpal blade went snicker-snack!
He left it dead, and with its head
  He went galumphing back.

"And hast thou slain the Jabberwock?
    Come to my arms, my beamish boy!
O frabjous day! Callooh! Callay!"
    He chortled in his joy.

94

'Twas brillig, and the slithy toves
  Did gyre and gimble in the wabe:
All mimsy were the borogoves,
  And the mome raths outgrabe.

Lewis Carroll

95

Witch Work

The witch was as old as the mulberry tree
She lived in the house of a hundred clocks
She sold storms and sorrows and calmed the sea
And she kept her life in a box

The tree was the oldest that I'd ever seen
Its trunk flowed like liquid. It dripped with age.
But every September its fruit stained the green
As scarlet as harlots,
As red as my rage.

The clocks whispered time which they caught in their gears
They crept and they chattered, they chimed and they chewed.
She fed them on minutes. The old ones ate years.
She feared and she loved them
Her wild clocky brood.

She sold me a storm
When my anger was strong
And my hate filled the world with volcanoes and laughter
I watched as the lightnings and wind sang their song
And my madness was swallowed by what happened after.

She sold me three sorrows—all wrapped in a cloth.
The first one I gave to my enemy's child.
The second my woman made into a broth.
The third waits unused, for we reconciled.

She sold calm seas to the mariners' wives
Bound the winds with silk cords so the storms could be tied there.
The women at home lived much happier lives,
Till their husbands returned, and their patience be tried there.

101

The witch hid her life in a box made of dirt,
As big as a fist and as dark as a heart.
There was nothing but time there and silence and hurt
While the witch watched the waves with her pain and her art.

But he never came back.
He never came back . . .

The witch was as old as the mulberry tree
She lived in the house of a hundred clocks
She sold storms and sorrows and calmed the sea
And she kept her life in a box.

Neil Gaiman

103

The Listeners

"Is there anybody there?" said the Traveller,
  Knocking on the moonlit door;
And his horse in the silence champed the grasses
  Of the forest's ferny floor:
And a bird flew up out of the turret,
  Above the Traveller's head:
And he smote upon the door again a second time;
  "Is there anybody there?" he said.
But no one descended to the Traveller;
  No head from the leaf-fringed sill
Leaned over and looked into his grey eyes,
  Where he stood perplexed and still.
But only a host of phantom listeners
  That dwelt in the lone house then
Stood listening in the quiet of the moonlight
  To that voice from the world of men:
Stood thronging the faint moonbeams on the dark stair,
  That goes down to the empty hall,
Hearkening in an air stirred and shaken
  By the lonely Traveller's call.
And he felt in his heart their strangeness,
  Their stillness answering his cry,
While his horse moved, cropping the dark turf,

'Neath the starred and leafy sky;
For he suddenly smote on the door, even
   Louder, and lifted his head:—
"Tell them I came, and no one answered,
   That I kept my word," he said.
Never the least stir made the listeners,
   Though every word he spake
Fell echoing through the shadowiness of the still house
   From the one man left awake:
Ay, they heard his foot upon the stirrup,
   And the sound of iron on stone,
And how the silence surged softly backward,
   When the plunging hoofs were gone.

Walter de la Mare

Orphee

Orpheus was a musician. He made songs. He knew mysteries. One day the panther girls high on wine and lust came past and tore him flesh from flesh. His head still sang and prophesied as it floated down to the sea.

(Do not look back. Do not look back.)

There was a girl, and he said she was his girl. He followed her to
Hell when she died. You could do that when your girlfriend dies:
there are entrances to Hell in every major city: so many doors,
who has time to look behind each one?

When Orpheus was young he got the girl back from Hell safely.
That's where the years came from. Euridice comes home from
Hell and the flowers bloom and the world puddles and quickens,
and it's Spring.

But that was never good enough.

And before that Spring story, it was a life and death tale. We got a million of them. If he hadn't looked back, if he just hadn't looked back, then all the people would come back from the dead all the time, each of us, no more ghosts, no more darkness.

I would go to Hell to see you once more. There's a door on the third floor of the New York Public Library, on the way to the men's toilets, by the little Charles Addams gallery. It's never locked. You just have to open it. I would go to Hell for you. I would tell them stories that are not false and that are not true. I would tell them stories until they wept salt tears and gave you back to me and to the world.

It doesn't have to be a year. I'd take a day. I'd take an hour. I'd walk in front of you to the light.

But I'd look back, wouldn't I? We all would. The ones who can't look back, who can only stare into the sunrise ahead of them, stare into the glorious future, those people don't get to visit Hell.

So Orpheus came back and carried on, because he had to, and he made magic and sang songs. He taught that there was only truth in dreams. That was one of the mysteries: in dreams the veil was lifted and you could see so far forward you might as well have been looking back.

Some die in Washington DC or in London or in Mexico. They do not look forward to their deaths. They glance aside, or down, or they look back. Every hour wounds. That was what she told me. Every hour wounds, the last one kills.

115

And looking back now, she's standing naked in the moonlight.
Her breast is already blackening, her body a feast of tiny wounds.
Izanagi followed his wife to the shadow lands, but he looked back:
he saw her face, her dead face, and he fled.

I dreamed today of bone-white horses, stamping and nuzzling in the bright sunshine, and of orange poppies which swayed and danced in the spring wind.

(Do not look back.)

She had the softest lips, he said. He said, she had the softest lips of all. And her head still sang and prophesied as it floated down to the sea.

Neil Gaiman

The Lady of Shalott

Part I
On either side the river lie
Long fields of barley and of rye,
That clothe the wold and meet the sky;
And thro' the field the road runs by
    To many-tower'd Camelot;
The yellow-leaved waterlily
The green-sheathed daffodilly
Tremble in the water chilly
    Round about Shalott.

120

Willows whiten, aspens shiver.
The sunbeam showers break and quiver
In the stream that runneth ever
By the island in the river
    Flowing down to Camelot.
Four gray walls, and four gray towers
Overlook a space of flowers,
And the silent isle imbowers
    The Lady of Shalott.

121

Underneath the bearded barley,
The reaper, reaping late and early,
Hears her ever chanting cheerly,
Like an angel, singing clearly,
   O'er the stream of Camelot.
Piling the sheaves in furrows airy,
Beneath the moon, the reaper weary
Listening whispers, "'Tis the fairy
   Lady of Shalott."

The little isle is all inrail'd
With a rose-fence, and overtrail'd
With roses: by the marge unhail'd
The shallop flitteth silken sail'd,
    Skimming down to Camelot.
A pearl garland winds her head:
She leaneth on a velvet bed,
Full royally apparelled,
    The Lady of Shalott.

123

Part II

No time hath she to sport and play:
A charmed web she weaves alway.
A curse is on her, if she stay
Her weaving, either night or day,
    To look down to Camelot.
She knows not what the curse may be;
Therefore she weaveth steadily,
Therefore no other care hath she,
    The Lady of Shalott.

124

She lives with little joy or fear.
Over the water, running near,
The sheepbell tinkles in her ear.
Before her hangs a mirror clear,
    Reflecting tower'd Camelot.
And as the mazy web she whirls,
She sees the surly village churls,
And the red cloaks of market girls
    Pass onward from Shalott.

Sometimes a troop of damsels glad,
An abbot on an ambling pad,
Sometimes a curly shepherd lad,
Or long-hair'd page in crimson clad,
    Goes by to tower'd Camelot:
And sometimes thro' the mirror blue
The knights come riding two and two:
She hath no loyal knight and true,
    The Lady of Shalott.

But in her web she still delights
To weave the mirror's magic sights,
For often thro' the silent nights
A funeral, with plumes and lights
    And music, came from Camelot:
Or when the moon was overhead
Came two young lovers lately wed;
"I am half sick of shadows," said
    The Lady of Shalott.

Part III

A bow-shot from her bower-eaves,
He rode between the barley-sheaves,
The sun came dazzling thro' the leaves,
And flam'd upon the brazen greaves
  Of bold Sir Lancelot.
A red-cross knight for ever kneel'd
To a lady in his shield,
That sparkled on the yellow field,
  Beside remote Shalott.

The gemmy bridle glitter'd free,
Like to some branch of stars we see
Hung in the golden Galaxy.
The bridle bells rang merrily
    As he rode down from Camelot:
And from his blazon'd baldric slung
A mighty silver bugle hung,
And as he rode his armour rung,
    Beside remote Shalott.

129

All in the blue unclouded weather
Thick-jewell'd shone the saddle-leather,
The helmet and the helmet-feather
Burn'd like one burning flame together,
    As he rode down from Camelot.
As often thro' the purple night,
Below the starry clusters bright,
Some bearded meteor, trailing light,
    Moves over green Shalott.

His broad clear brow in sunlight glow'd;
On burnish'd hooves his war-horse trode;
From underneath his helmet flow'd
His coal-black curls as on he rode,
    As he rode down from Camelot.
From the bank and from the river
He flash'd into the crystal mirror,
"Tirra lirra, tirra lirra,"
    Sang Sir Lancelot.

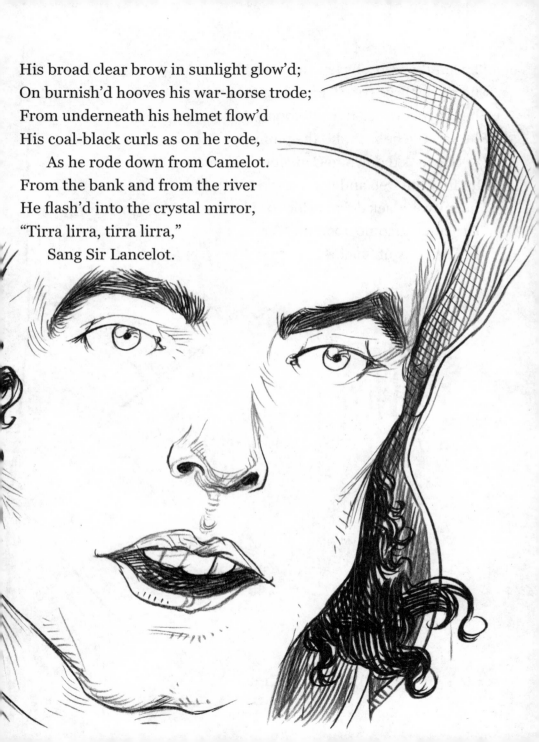

She left the web, she left the loom
She made three paces thro' the room
She saw the water-flower bloom,
She saw the helmet and the plume,
    She look'd down to Camelot.
Out flew the web and floated wide;
The mirror crack'd from side to side;
"The curse is come upon me," cried
    The Lady of Shalott.

Part IV

In the stormy east-wind straining,
The pale yellow woods were waning,
The broad stream in his banks complaining,
Heavily the low sky raining
    Over tower'd Camelot;
Outside the isle a shallow boat
Beneath a willow lay afloat,
Below the carven stern she wrote,
    The Lady of Shalott.

A cloud-white crown of pearl she dight,
All raimented in snowy white
That loosely flew (her zone in sight
Clasp'd with one blinding diamond bright)
    Her wide eyes fix'd on Camelot,
Though the squally east-wind keenly
Blew, with folded arms serenely
By the water stood the queenly
    Lady of Shalott.

134

With a steady stony glance—
Like some bold seer in a trance,
Beholding all his own mischance,
Mute, with a glassy countenance—
    She look'd down to Camelot.
It was the closing of the day:
She loos'd the chain, and down she lay;
The broad stream bore her far away,
    The Lady of Shalott.

As when to sailors while they roam,
By creeks and outfalls far from home,
Rising and dropping with the foam,
From dying swans wild warblings come,
    Blown shoreward; so to Camelot
Still as the boathead wound along
The willowy hills and fields among,
They heard her chanting her death-song,
    The Lady of Shalott.

A long-drawn carol, mournful, holy,
She chanted loudly, chanted lowly,
Till her eyes were darken'd wholly,
And her smooth face sharpen'd slowly,
 Turn'd to tower'd Camelot:
For ere she reach'd upon the tide
The first house by the water-side,
Singing in her song she died,
 The Lady of Shalott.

Under tower and balcony,
By garden wall and gallery,
A pale, pale corpse she floated by,
Dead-cold, between the houses high,
  Dead into tower'd Camelot.
Knight and burgher, lord and dame,
To the planked wharfage came:
Below the stern they read her name,
  The Lady of Shalott.

They cross'd themselves, their stars they blest,
Knight, minstrel, abbot, squire, and guest.
There lay a parchment on her breast,
That puzzled more than all the rest,
    The wellfed wits at Camelot.
"The web was woven curiously,
The charm is broken utterly,
Draw near and fear not,—this is I,
    The Lady of Shalott."

Alfred, Lord Tennyson

NATURE

Ode to a Nightingale

My heart aches, and a drowsy numbness pains
     My sense, as though of hemlock I had drunk,
Or emptied some dull opiate to the drains
     One minute past, and Lethe-wards had sunk:
'Tis not through envy of thy happy lot,
     But being too happy in thine happiness,—
        That thou, light-winged Dryad of the trees
           In some melodious plot
     Of beechen green, and shadows numberless,
        Singest of summer in full-throated ease.

142

O, for a draught of vintage! that hath been
    Cool'd a long age in the deep-delved earth,
Tasting of Flora and the country green,
    Dance, and Provençal song, and sunburnt mirth!
O for a beaker full of the warm South,
    Full of the true, the blushful Hippocrene,
      With beaded bubbles winking at the brim,
        And purple-stained mouth;
That I might drink, and leave the world unseen,
    And with thee fade away into the forest dim:

Fade far away, dissolve, and quite forget
  What thou among the leaves hast never known,
The weariness, the fever, and the fret
  Here, where men sit and hear each other groan;
Where palsy shakes a few, sad, last gray hairs,
  Where youth grows pale, and spectre-thin, and dies;
    Where but to think is to be full of sorrow
      And leaden-eyed despairs,
Where Beauty cannot keep her lustrous eyes,
  Or new Love pine at them beyond to-morrow.

Away! away! for I will fly to thee,
    Not charioted by Bacchus and his pards,
But on the viewless wings of Poesy,
    Though the dull brain perplexes and retards:
Already with thee! tender is the night,
    And haply the Queen-Moon is on her throne,
        Cluster'd around by all her starry Fays;
            But here there is no light,
Save what from heaven is with the breezes blown
    Through verdurous glooms and winding mossy ways.

I cannot see what flowers are at my feet,
　　Nor what soft incense hangs upon the boughs,
But, in embalmed darkness, guess each sweet
　　Wherewith the seasonable month endows
The grass, the thicket, and the fruit-tree wild;
　　White hawthorn, and the pastoral eglantine;
　　　Fast fading violets cover'd up in leaves;
　　　　And mid-May's eldest child,
　　The coming musk-rose, full of dewy wine,
　　　The murmurous haunt of flies on summer eves.

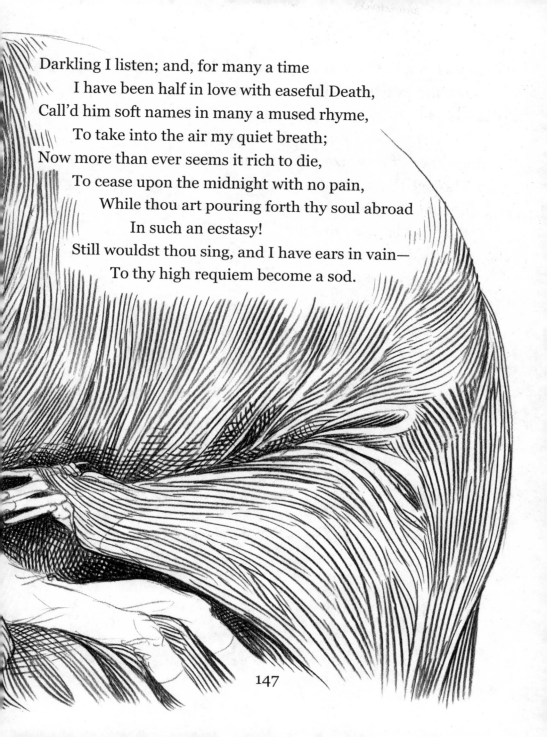

Darkling I listen; and, for many a time
    I have been half in love with easeful Death,
Call'd him soft names in many a mused rhyme,
    To take into the air my quiet breath;
Now more than ever seems it rich to die,
    To cease upon the midnight with no pain,
      While thou art pouring forth thy soul abroad
        In such an ecstasy!
    Still wouldst thou sing, and I have ears in vain—
      To thy high requiem become a sod.

Thou wast not born for death, immortal Bird!
    No hungry generations tread thee down;
The voice I hear this passing night was heard
    In ancient days by emperor and clown:
Perhaps the self-same song that found a path
        Through the sad heart of Ruth, when, sick for home,
            She stood in tears amid the alien corn;
                The same that oft-times hath
        Charm'd magic casements, opening on the foam
        Of perilous seas, in faery lands forlorn.

Forlorn! the very word is like a bell
    To toll me back from thee to my sole self!
Adieu! the fancy cannot cheat so well
    As she is fam'd to do, deceiving elf.
Adieu! adieu! thy plaintive anthem fades
    Past the near meadows, over the still stream,
        Up the hill-side; and now 'tis buried deep
            In the next valley-glades:
    Was it a vision, or a waking dream?
        Fled is that music:—Do I wake or sleep?

John Keats

Moon-Whales

They plough through the moon stuff
Just under the surface
Lifting the moon's skin
Like a muscle
But so slowly it seems like a lasting mountain
Breathing so rarely it seems like a volcano
Leaving a hole blasted in the moon's skin

Sometimes they plunge deep
Under the moon's plains
Making their magnetic way
Through the moon's interior metals
Sending the astronaut's instruments scatty.

Their music is immense
Each note hundreds of years long
Each whole tune a moon-age

So they sing to each other unending songs
As unmoving they move their immovable masses

Their eyes closed ecstatic

Ted Hughes

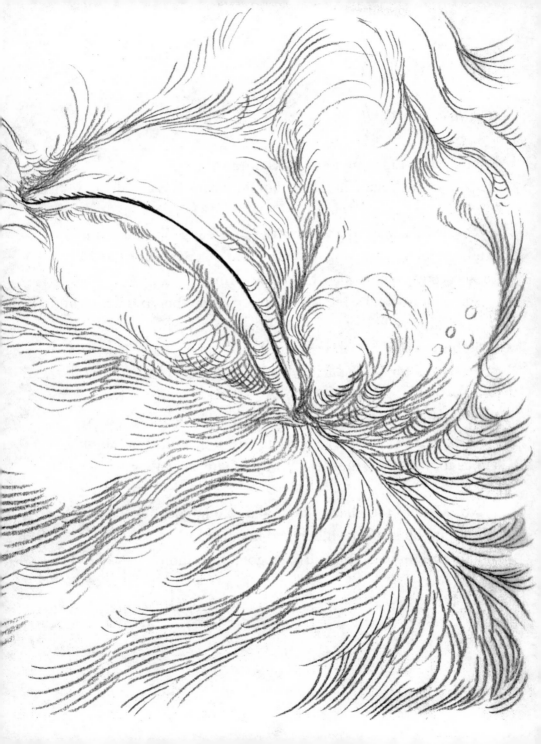

The Windhover

To Christ our Lord

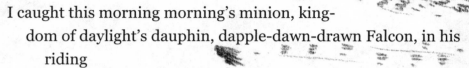

I caught this morning morning's minion, king-
  dom of daylight's dauphin, dapple-dawn-drawn Falcon, in his
    riding
  Of the rolling level underneath him steady air, and striding
High there, how he rung upon the rein of a wimpling wing
In his ecstasy! then off, off forth on swing,
  As a skate's heel sweeps smooth on a bow-bend: the hurl and
    gliding
  Rebuffed the big wind. My heart in hiding
Stirred for a bird,—the achieve of, the mastery of the thing!

Brute beauty and valour and act, oh, air, pride, plume, here
  Buckle! AND the fire that breaks from thee then, a billion
Times told lovelier, more dangerous, O my chevalier!

  No wonder of it: shéer plód makes plough down sillion
Shine, and blue-bleak embers, ah my dear,
  Fall, gall themselves, and gash gold-vermilion.

Gerard Manley Hopkins

152

The Language of Cat

Teach me the language of Cat;
the slow-motion blink, that crystal stare,
a tight-lipped purr and a wide-mouthed hiss.
Let me walk with a saunter, nose in the air.

Teach my ears the way to ignore
names that I'm called. May they only twitch
to the distant shake of a boxful of biscuits,
the clink of a fork on a china dish.

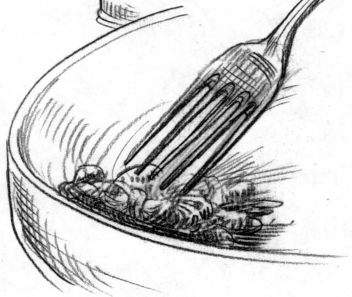

Teach me that vanishing trick
where dents in cushions appear, and I'm missed.
Show me the high-wire trip along fences
To hideaway places, that no one but me knows exist.

Don't teach me Dog,
all eager to please; that slobbers, yaps and begs for a pat,
that sits when told by its owner, that's led on a lead.
No, not that. Teach me the language of Cat.

Rachel Rooney

157

WAR

Dulce et Decorum Est

Bent double, like old beggars under sacks,
Knock-kneed, coughing like hags, we cursed through sludge,
Till on the haunting flares we turned our backs
And towards our distant rest began to trudge.
Men marched asleep. Many had lost their boots,
But limped on, blood-shod. All went lame; all blind;
Drunk with fatigue; deaf even to the hoots
Of gas-shells dropping softly behind.

Gas! GAS! Quick, boys!—An ecstasy of fumbling,
Fitting the clumsy helmets just in time;
But someone still was yelling out and stumbling,
And flound'ring like a man in fire or lime . . .
Dim through the misty panes and thick green light,
As under a green sea, I saw him drowning.

In all my dreams, before my helpless sight,
He plunges at me, guttering, choking, drowning.

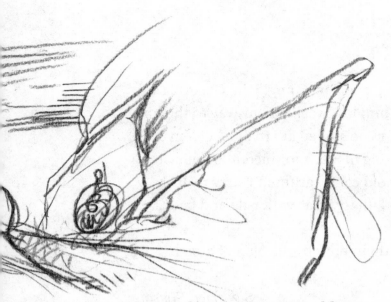

If in some smothering dreams you too could pace
Behind the wagon that we flung him in,
And watch the white eyes writhing in his face,
His hanging face, like a devil's sick of sin;
If you could hear, at every jolt, the blood
Come gargling from the froth-corrupted lungs,
Obscene as cancer, bitter as the cud
Of vile, incurable sores on innocent tongues,—
My friend, you would not tell with such high zest
To children ardent for some desperate glory,
The old Lie: *Dulce et decorum est*
Pro patria mori.

Wilfred Owen

The General

"Good-morning, good-morning!" the General said
When we met him last week on our way to the line.
Now the soldiers he smiled at are most of 'em dead,
And we're cursing his staff for incompetent swine.
"He's a cheery old card," grunted Harry to Jack
As they slogged up to Arras with rifle and pack.

But he did for them both by his plan of attack.

Siegfried Sassoon

There Will Come Soft Rains

(War Time)

There will come soft rains and the smell of the ground,
And swallows circling with their shimmering sound;

And frogs in the pools singing at night,
And wild plum-trees in tremulous white;

Robins will wear their feathery fire
Whistling their whims on a low fence-wire;

And not one will know of the war, not one
Will care at last when it is done.

Not one would mind, neither bird nor tree
If mankind perished utterly;

And Spring herself, when she woke at dawn,
Would scarcely know that we were gone.

Sara Teasdale

ENDINGS

Not Waving but Drowning

Nobody heard him, the dead man,
But still he lay moaning:
I was much further out than you thought
And not waving but drowning.

Poor chap, he always loved larking
And now he's dead
It must have been too cold for him his heart gave way,
They said.

Oh, no no no, it was too cold always
(Still the dead one lay moaning)
I was much too far out all my life
And not waving but drowning.

Stevie Smith

Let Me Die a Youngman's Death

Let me die a youngman's death
not a clean and inbetween
the sheets holywater death
not a famous-last-words
peaceful out of breath death

When I'm 73
and in constant good tumour
may I be mown down at dawn
by a bright red sports car
on my way home
from an allnight party

Or when I'm 91
with silver hair
and sitting in a barber's chair
may rival gangsters
with hamfisted tommyguns burst in
and give me a short back and insides

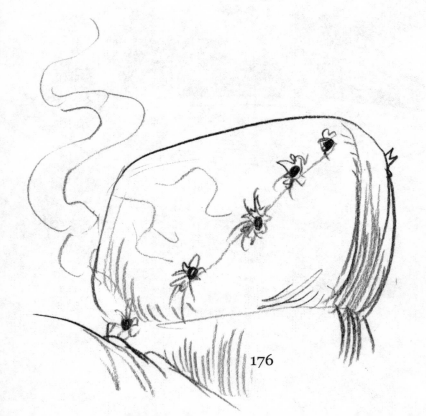

Or when I'm 104
and banned from the Cavern
may my mistress
catching me in bed with her daughter
and fearing for her son
cut me up into little pieces
and throw away every piece but one

Let me die a youngman's death
not a free from sin tiptoe in
candle wax and waning death
not a curtains drawn by angels borne
"what a nice way to go" death

Roger McGough

Do Not Go Gentle into That Good Night

Do not go gentle into that good night,
Old age should burn and rave at close of day;
Rage, rage against the dying of the light.

Though wise men at their end know dark is right,
Because their words had forked no lightning they
Do not go gentle into that good night.

Good men, the last wave by, crying how bright
Their frail deeds might have danced in a green bay,
Rage, rage against the dying of the light.

Wild men who caught and sang the sun in flight,
And learn, too late, they grieved it on its way,
Do not go gentle into that good night.

Grave men, near death, who see with blinding sight
Blind eyes could blaze like meteors and be gay,
Rage, rage against the dying of the light.

And you, my father, there on the sad height,
Curse, bless, me now with your fierce tears,
  I pray.
Do not go gentle into that good night.
Rage, rage against the dying of the light.

Dylan Thomas

181

Because I could not stop for Death

Because I could not stop for Death—
He kindly stopped for me—
The Carriage held but just Ourselves—
And Immortality.

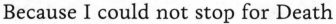

We slowly drove—He knew no haste
And I had put away
My labor and my leisure too,
For His Civility—

We passed the School, where Children strove
At Recess—in the Ring—
We passed the Fields of Gazing Grain—
We passed the Setting Sun—

184

Or rather—He passed Us—
The Dews drew quivering and chill—
For only Gossamer, my Gown—
My Tippet—only Tulle—

185

We paused before a House that seemed
A Swelling of the Ground—
The Roof was scarcely visible—
The Cornice—in the Ground—

Since then—'tis Centuries—and yet
Feels shorter than the Day
I first surmised the Horses' Heads
Were toward Eternity—

Emily Dickinson

187

"To be, or not to be"

from *Hamlet*

To be, or not to be—that is the question:
Whether 'tis nobler in the mind to suffer
The slings and arrows of outrageous fortune,
Or to take arms against a sea of troubles
And by opposing end them. To die—to sleep,
No more—and by a sleep to say we end
The heartache and the thousand natural shocks
That flesh is heir to. 'Tis a consummation
Devoutly to be wished. To die, to sleep—
To sleep, perchance to dream: ay, there's the rub,
For in that sleep of death what dreams may come
When we have shuffled off this mortal coil
Must give us pause. There's the respect
That makes calamity of so long life.
For who would bear the whips and scorns of time,
Th' oppressor's wrong, the proud man's contumely
The pangs of despised love, the law's delay,
The insolence of office, and the spurns
That patient merit of th' unworthy takes,
When he himself might his quietus make
With a bare bodkin? Who would fardels bear,
To grunt and sweat under a weary life,

But that the dread of something after death,
The undiscovered country, from whose bourn
No traveller returns, puzzles the will,
And makes us rather bear those ills we have
Than fly to others that we know not of?
Thus conscience does make cowards of us all,
And thus the native hue of resolution
Is sicklied o'er with the pale cast of thought,
And enterprises of great pitch and moment
With this regard their currents turn awry
And lose the name of action.

William Shakespeare

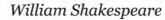

"Tomorrow, and tomorrow, and tomorrow"
from *Macbeth*

Tomorrow, and tomorrow, and tomorrow,
Creeps in this petty pace from day to day,
To the last syllable of recorded time;
And all our yesterdays have lighted fools
The way to dusty death. Out, out, brief candle!
Life's but a walking shadow, a poor player,
That struts and frets his hour upon the stage,
And then is heard no more. It is a tale
Told by an idiot, full of sound and fury,
Signifying nothing.

William Shakespeare

Index of First Lines

Index of Poets

Acknowledgments

The compiler and publisher would like to thank the following for permission to use their copyright material:

Armitage, Simon: "I am very bothered" from *Book of Matches* (Faber and Faber, 2001). Copyright © Simon Armitage. Used by permission of the agent; **Bridgers, Phoebe:** "Smoke Signals" written by Phoebe Bridgers (Whatever Mom) Copyright © Whatever Mom. Administered by Kobalt Music Publishing Ltd. Used with permission of the publisher; **Causley, Charles:** "Eden Rock" from *Collected Poems 1951–2000* (Macmillan, 2000). Copyright © the Estate of Charles Causley. Used by permission of David Higham Associates; **Cave, Nick:** "Love Letter" written by Nick Cave and published by Mute Song Limited. Copyright © Mute Song. Used with permission of the publisher; **Cohen, Leonard:** "Suzanne" by Leonard Cohen. Copyright © 1993, Leonard Cohen and Leonard Cohen Stranger Music, Inc. Used by permission of The Wylie Agency (UK) Limited; **Day Lewis, Cecil:** "Walking Away" from *Selected Poems* by Cecil Day Lewis. Copyright © the Estate of Cecil Day Lewis. Reprinted by permission of Peters Fraser & Dunlop (www.petersfraserdunlop.com) on behalf of the Estate of Cecil Day Lewis; **Dharker, Imtiaz:** "Tissue" from *The Terrorist at my Table* (Bloodaxe Books, 2006). Copyright © Imtiaz Dharker. Used by permission of the publisher; **Duffy, Carol Ann:** "Safe Sounds" from *New and Collected Poems for Children* (Faber and Faber, 2009) and "Valentine" from *New Selected Poems 1984–2004* (Picador, 2011). Copyright © Carol Ann Duffy. Reproduced by permission of the author c/o Rogers, Coleridge & White., 20 Powis Mews, London W11 1JN; **Gaiman, Neil:** "Witch work" first published in *Under My Hat: Tales from the Cauldron* (Bluefire, 2013) and "Orphee" first published by BBC Radio 4 (2015). Copyright © Neil Gaiman. Reprinted by permission of Writers House LLC acting as agent for the author; **Harrold, A. F.:** "I Miss You" first published in *Things You Find in a Poets Beard* (Burning Eye Books, 2015). Copyright © A. F. Harrold. Reproduced by kind permission of the poet; **Heaney, Seamus:** "Digging" from *Opened Ground: Selected Poems 1966–1996* (Farrar, Straus and Giroux, 1998). Copyright © Seamus Heaney. Reproduced by permission of Farrar, Straus & Giroux; **Hughes, Ted:** "Moon-whales" from *Collected Poems for Children* (Farrar, Straus and Giroux BYR, 2007).

About Chris Riddell

Chis Riddell is an accomplished artist, writer, and political cartoonist for the *Observer*. He has been called the "greatest illustrator of his generation" and has received many awards for his work, including the Kate Greenaway Medal three times, the Costa Children's Book Award, and the Hay Festival Medal for Illustration. From 2015 to 2017, he served as the UK Children's Laureate, and in 2019 he received an OBE (Officer of the Most Excellent Order of the British Empire) from Queen Elizabeth II in recognition of his illustration and charity work. Chris lives in Brighton, England, with his family. You can find him online @chris_ridell on Instagram and @chrisriddell50 on Twitter.